# ANNA WITCH

# ANNA WITCH

By

MADELEINE EDMONDSON

ILLUSTRATIONS BY

William Pène du Bois

DOUBLEDAY & COMPANY, INC.
GARDEN CITY, NEW YORK

Library of Congress Cataloging in Publication Data

Edmondson, Madeleine.
Anna Witch.

Summary: A little witch girl makes a discovery about life without mother after a loss of temper clashes with a loss of patience.
[1. Witches—Fiction. 2. Mothers and daughters—Fiction]
I. Du Bois, William Pène, 1916– ill.
II. Title
PZ7.E2475An [Fic]
AACR2
ISBN: 0-385-17393-8 Trade
ISBN: 0-385-17394-6 Prebound
Library of Congress Catalog Card Number: 81–43653



BOOK DESIGN BY BENTE HAMANN
Printed in the United States of America

*First Edition*

*For Clem*

# ANNA WITCH

# CHAPTER 1

Once upon a time, and not so very long ago either, a big witch and a little witch lived together in a gingerbread-and-candy house deep in the dark forest. The little one was named Anna Witch, because witches are very fond of names that spell the same forward and backward. Her mother's name was Ada Witch, but sometimes Anna called her Mom, because that spells the same both ways too. Around their house was a white picket fence with a magic gate that opened only when Anna Witch or her mother asked it to.

They were both very beautiful, as witches go, though witches do not judge beauty in quite the same way we do. For one thing, their hair does not hang down like ours but floats upward from their heads. That is why they wear such tall hats. Witches have chicken feet and pointed ears, and their skin is a very light green. Anna Witch and Ada Witch were no exception to this rule.

The two of them lived alone except for their pet owl, whose name was Otto. Otto was very old, and of course very wise. By day he dozed in the house, but he spent his nights flying about in the forest. Because he could see in the dark, he knew the places where golden treasures are buried, the hollow trees where the squirrels hide their nuts, and the secret nests where the snakes lay their eggs. And all night long he gathered sticks for the fire Ada Witch made every morning under her big black witch's pot.

Anna Witch and her mother lived a very pleasant life in their little gingerbread house. In the morning they had lessons. Ada Witch taught Anna how to do magic. At lunchtime Ada Witch would clap her hands and a little magic table would appear, laden with all kinds of good things to eat—things that witches love, like tadpole soup and grasshopper sausage. When they had eaten their fill, she would clap her hands again and make the little table vanish, so they hardly ever had to wash dishes.

Most afternoons, Anna Witch went out to play in the forest while her mother was busy at home. Ada Witch had a lot to do. She tended her herb garden. She baked cakes and cookies in the brick oven beside the fireplace. She sewed and embroidered clothes for herself and Anna Witch. And, of course, she was forever brewing all kinds of potions and philters and medicines in her big black caldron, as witches have always liked to do. Sometimes she let Anna Witch help with the baking. And sometimes they would stir up a batch of frosting to spread on the outside of the house to keep it nice and white.

But every evening when work was done and the sun was setting behind the mountain, the two of them would pack a picnic basket, dress in their best, put on their tall, pointed hats, and climb onto their broomsticks. Ada Witch on her big broom and Anna Witch on her little one, they flew up to the mountaintop where all

the country witches meet each night. The motherwitches gossip and trade the latest spells, and they all dance around their bonfire and sing the old songs that have been handed down among the witches from the beginning of time. The witchdaughters, like Anna, play games like leaplizard, pass-the-toadstool, and skipsnake, and enjoy themselves until it is time for the midnight picnic.

You can see that Anna's life was a very nice one indeed, but she was not always happy. Sometimes, in fact, Anna Witch was very unhappy and cross. Witches, as a rule, are calm and seldom lose their tempers, but you must remember that Anna was a very young witch.

The truth is that Anna Witch could not learn to do magic. Every morning Ada Witch got out the big magic book and gave Anna a lesson in spell casting. But though she herself was a very clever witch, she was not a good teacher. She had spent months trying to teach Anna how to turn milk sour just by looking at it in a certain way. But Anna still couldn't do it every time she tried. Ada Witch had given up trying to show her daughter how to turn people into frogs and even how to transform pebbles into pearls. All these things were too

about. Today you're going to learn to make yourself disappear."

"Oh," said Anna Witch, losing interest.

"You see, Anna," her mother explained, "there's a great difference between creating something and transporting someone. And there's an even greater difference between either of those things and the spell you're going to learn today. This spell makes things—or people—disappear. Then the next spell makes them appear again." Ada Witch stopped talking and looked at Anna Witch. "Anna, are you listening to me?"

"Yes," said Anna, looking out the window.

"Did you understand what I was saying?"

"Of course," said Anna.

"For instance," Ada Witch went on, "I could make this book disappear. See?" And with a quick spell from Ada Witch the big magic book was gone. Then a wave of the hand, another quick spell, and the book was back on the table again. "You see how easy that was?"

"Oh, do that again," said Anna, beginning to pay attention. She liked to see her mother do magic. It did look easy when Ada Witch did it. "Make something else disappear."

"All right," said Ada Witch, who always enjoyed showing off her magic powers. "What shall it be?"

Otto, who was napping on top of Ada Witch's spinning wheel in the corner, opened his eyes. "Whose lesson is this anyway?" he asked disapprovingly. "I thought Ada Witch already knew how to do all these simple tricks."

"Of course you're right, Otto," said Ada Witch, slightly shamefaced. "First Anna must learn the spell, and then I'll show her how to make herself disappear. You go back to sleep now."

The owl closed his eyes, and Ada Witch turned to Anna again. "Won't that be fun?" she said. Anna did not think it would be fun, but she did not say so.

The magic book was handwritten in faded brown ink. The capital letters and the borders of the pages were decorated with birds and animals painted in different colors. Anna enjoyed looking at the pictures; every time she looked at them she found something new and strange. But she did not read the spell.

Ada Witch sat at the other side of the table

with her embroidery. She always made new clothes for herself and her daughter for each holiday, and now she was getting ready for Lammas. Witch dresses are always black and rather plain, but for holidays a witch needs many embroidered petticoats so that when she dances a nice swirl of ruffles can be seen around her ankles.

After a while Ada Witch looked up from her embroidery. "Have you learned the spell by heart?" she asked.

"Yes," said Anna, "I think so."

"Very well," said her mother. "Get my silver mirror and I'll show you how it's done."

Anna ran and fetched the silver hand mirror. It was very heavy and its back and handle were carved with designs of leaves and flowers.

"Now watch carefully," said Ada Witch. "First I put my arms behind my back, and I hold my right elbow with my left hand, and my left elbow with my right. Then I gather all my powers and make the pupils of my eyes very small."

Anna looked at her mother's eyes and saw them changing into little black pinpoints. "How do you do that?" she asked.

"It comes with practice," her mother explained. "But at first there's an easy way. Just stare into a bright light, and you'll feel your eyes changing. Now look into the mirror and I'll make you invisible."

Anna watched her face in the mirror as her mother recited the spell:

"Smoke hides fire, mist hides moon.
Dark clouds hide the sun at noon.
Come hither, night, dissolve the light,
Hide Anna from all others' sight."

As Ada Witch said the spell, Anna felt odd little shooting pains in her hands and feet,. and she began to feel cold. As she grew colder and colder, she looked into the mirror and saw her own face dissolving. She held up her hand. She looked down at her little chicken feet. She wasn't there.

"I don't like this," she cried. "Quick, turn me back!" And sure enough, next minute there was her face in the mirror again.

"Now," said Ada Witch, "you try it. Of course, when you get to the last line of the spell, you say, 'Hide *me* from all others' sight,' just the way it's written in the book."

"I don't want to do it," said Anna. "I hate the way it feels."

"Being invisible does make you a little cold, I know," admitted Ada Witch, "but you get used to it."

"But I don't want to be invisible," protested Anna Witch. "If I were invisible, how would anybody know I was there?"

"It might be very useful someday," said Ada Witch. "And besides, this spell is the beginning of the chapter."

"Couldn't I practice making something else invisible?" suggested Anna.

"Anna dear," her mother explained, "the reason this spell is the first one in the chapter is that it's the easiest. Your powers are always strongest within yourself. But after you've learned to make yourself invisible, of course you can practice on other things."

"Even an owl must hop before it can fly," said Otto from his perch atop the spinning wheel. Anna pretended not to hear him.

"Now let me hear you recite the spell," said Ada Witch.

"I can't," said Anna. "I can't remember the words."

Ada Witch sighed. She got up from the table and folded her embroidery. "I'm going out to tend the garden," she announced. "And while I'm gone I want you to sit right there and practice that spell." She turned over the hourglass. "When all the sand has run through," she said, "you may go out to play."

Seed
Cakes

# CHAPTER 3

Anna began to try the spell. She stared into the fire until she was sure her eyes were pinpoints. Then she folded her arms behind her back and started to read the spell. She knew she was doing it partly right because she felt pins and needles in her feet, and she began to feel chilly. But it was not quite right, because when she looked into the silver mirror her face was still there.

Magic was so tiresome, Anna Witch thought to herself. How slowly the time was passing. She shook the hourglass, but the little grains of sand refused to go any faster. Out in the forest there were so many things to do. How she wished she were there.

She looked at the spell again. "Smoke hides fire, mist hides moon," she mumbled to herself, trying to learn it. And then she had an idea. What if instead of asking, "Hide *me* from all others' sight" she were to say, "Hide *Otto* from all others' sight"? That would be far more interesting!

She started again from the beginning, gathering all her powers, staring into the fire, clutching her elbows. This time she did not feel little twinges of cold, or prickling sensations in her hands and feet. In fact, she felt as if she were playing a game. And as she watched the sleeping owl, he began to fade. She could see through him as if he were just a picture of an owl painted on a very thin piece of cloth. The light from the fire shone between his feathers. And then he was gone. Anna Witch was so pleased with what she had done that she began to laugh.

The voice of the owl came from the spinning wheel. "Is it impossible to take a peaceful nap in this house?" Otto asked irritably. "What's going on around here? I'm freezing."

"I was practicing a spell. I've made you invisible," Anna explained. "It does feel cold."

"Then make me visible again," said the owl, "and don't just stand there wasting time."

"I'll try," said Anna. "It tells how to do it right here in the book."

"I'm in rather a hurry," snapped the owl.

"It's on the next page, I think," Anna said. "I'll figure it out."

"I'd prefer not to wait that long," said Otto, not at all politely. "Go fetch your mother."

Anna Witch ran to the garden where her mother was snipping herbs with her little gold scissors. It took Ada Witch no time at all to come in and make Otto visible again.

The owl's feathers were all fluffed up with anger. "I don't think it's too much to ask," he said, "simply to be left alone. I'm not a fussy owl, but I do like to get my rest."

"I'm sure Anna's very sorry she disturbed you," said Ada Witch. "Aren't you, Anna?"

"Yes, I'm sorry," said Anna Witch. "Can I go out now?"

Ada Witch, reaching out to stroke the owl's feathers. "I hope you're right about Anna."

"Of course I'm right," said the owl. "Owls are always right. Now let's have another of those delicious little cakes."

# CHAPTER 4

That night, as usual, Anna Witch and her mother packed their picnic basket and flew off to the mountaintop. While the motherwitches sat around the fire telling stories of long-ago days, the witchdaughters played in the pine grove. From the grove they could look up and see the flickering light of the distant fire, but they were too far away to hear the songs. Later, at midnight, they would hear the bell calling them to the picnic and the dancing that followed.

The witchdaughters had just finished a long game of leaplizard. Now they were resting and deciding what to do next.

"How about hide-and-sneak?" suggested

Anna Witch. She was particularly good at that, being small and able to hide in places nobody would ever think to look.

"That's a baby game," said LaVal, the tallest of the witchdaughters.

"I vote for triangles-and-pentagrams," said Eve. This had been the favorite game among the witchdaughters all spring. They had a diagram scratched on a flat stone at the edge of the grove, and a large collection of shiny black and white pebbles to play with.

"All right," said Anna Witch. "I'll throw first for the black side."

"You just want to play T-and-P because you always win," said LaVal. "I'm tired of it."

LaVal was not a good loser. She always wanted to play something she could win, and she always wanted to be the leader. Anna knew how she felt, because she often felt the same way.

"I'll tell you what we'll do," said LaVal. "We'll have a spelling bee!"

All the witchdaughters looked at her. None of them had ever heard of a spelling bee.

"What's that?" asked Anna Witch.

"It's something my mother told me about," explained LaVal, lowering her voice mysteriously. "It's something the witchdaughters used to do in her day. Of course, you have to be very good at spells or you can't do it."

Anna's heart sank. "How do you play it?" she asked.

"I'll explain," said LaVal, importantly. She liked being the center of attention. "We all stand in a circle, and someone is the leader. That person chooses a spell and does it, and then everyone has to follow. And whoever fails is out. Then we do another spell, and another, until there's only one of us left—and that one is the winner."

To Anna this did not sound like a game at all. In fact, it sounded just like lessons at home. "Maybe we shouldn't play this game," she said out loud. "My mother told me magic is never to be played with."

"I told you," LaVal said, "my mother said she played it herself. And besides, your mother will never know."

"It doesn't sound like much fun to me," said Anna Witch.

"It's fun if you know lots of spells," said LaVal. "Aren't you good at magic?"

"I'm very good at it," said Anna Witch firmly.

"What spells are you studying?" asked LaVal.

"I just finished the chapter on appearances and disappearances," lied Anna.

"Oh, that's a hard one," said Nan. "I had an awful time with that."

"Appearances and disappearances are just baby magic," said LaVal. "Wait till you get to necromancy."

Anna had never even heard of necromancy. It must be much further ahead in the book. But she nodded as if she knew all about it. Perhaps, she thought to herself, she should ask to be the leader in this game. Then she would be the one to decide what spells they would do. Though, to be truthful, she couldn't think of any spells she was really sure of. Some of them might work—but then again, they might very well not.

But it was too late to be the leader. LaVal was already forming a circle and telling everyone where to stand.

"The spelling bee has begun," announced LaVal. "We'll do all the spells in a whisper, and don't stand too close. I'll announce the spell and then you'll have a count of thirteen. If you can't do it in that time, you're out."

Anna felt her palms getting damp.

"We'll start with an easy one and work our way up to harder and harder spells," LaVal continued. "You'll like round one, Anna. It will be a simple disappearance. Here I go."

Anna watched LaVal as hard as she could, but though the moon was shining brightly, she couldn't see much. She knew LaVal must be gathering her powers. She could see her lips moving. She saw her begin to fade. And then LaVal's place in the circle was empty.

But her voice was still there. "Next," said the voice. "It's your turn, Eve. I'll count." The empty space in the circle began to count to thirteen. "One, two, three, four, five, six, seven . . ."

Anna could see Eve growing paler, beginning to disappear. There were only four more turns before hers, and then she would have to do the spell. How did it begin? She tried to remember that morning and how the faded brown letters looked on the page.

She would start gathering her powers right away. Make the pupils of your eyes very small. Looking into a bright light will help. She stared as hard as she could into the only light there was, the distant bonfire. Remember how

it was done, both arms behind back, right hand on left elbow, left hand on right elbow. She knew she was trying as hard as she could—and it was her turn.

The voice of LaVal was counting again. "One, two, three . . ." Anna Witch felt a prickling in her hands and feet, and she began to shiver. Had she disappeared? Was she gone? She was afraid to look down. And then she heard LaVal's voice saying, "All right, Pip, it's your turn. One, two, three, four . . ." She must have disappeared. A great tide of relief flowed through Anna Witch's body as she looked down at her invisible feet.

ong to enjoy her
w minutes every
had managed to
o the pine grove
ing there but the

voice of LaVal.
eappear. Watch
e where LaVal
omething begin-
curly red hair,
en, in between,
LaVal looking
a felt a great

'al, and began
counting rather
LaVal reached
her. Soon, all
urn—and then

the morning.
pearing? Ada
bear, and she
Anna had not
uld not recall
L
ho
spell on the

same page as the disappearance spell? Rack her brains as she might, Anna could not remember.

All the other witchdaughters were reappearing, one after another, but since they were invisible Anna Witch could not see what, if anything, they were doing, and all she could hear was a buzz and a whisper.

And now it was her turn. Everyone was looking toward her. Of course they couldn't see her, and she was glad they couldn't.

"Your turn, Anna," said LaVal, and she started to count.

Anna tried. She willed herself to be visible. She wished with all her heart to become part of the circle again. But it was no use. LaVal had finished counting to thirteen. Everyone was waiting.

"Well," said LaVal, with an unfriendly laugh, "you're the first one out, Anna. Go and sit on the rock while we do the next round."

Anna did not want to sit on the rock and be the first one out. She did not like to be laughed at, and she did not like to lose. Then an idea came to her. No one had to know that she couldn't do the spell. She would just sneak quietly away. She would go and ask her mother to make her visible again. Then she would come back, and the other witchdaughters would never be the wiser.

Careful not to make a sound, Anna stepped out of the circle. Slowly she crept away from the circle of witchdaughters until she was at the very edge of the pine grove. Then she turned back to listen. They were talking about her.

"She's probably gone to tell her mother," LaVal was saying. "I knew we shouldn't let her play."

"Anna's not a tattletale," said Pip. Anna had never liked Pip very much, but now she changed her mind.

"Maybe we'd better play something else," said LaVal. "In case they come to see what we're doing."

"I didn't think spelling bee was a very good game anyhow," said Eve. "Let's collect some spider webs and play cat's cradle."

Anna had reached the foot of the rocky path up to the peak, and she climbed as fast as she could. She was too far away for the witch-daughters to hear her now. Eve was right. Spelling bee wasn't a good game at all. She would never, never play it again.

# CHAPTER 5

The motherwitches were sitting around the dying fire, listening as the oldest of the witches played her harp and sang a song with many verses. Anna could not understand it because the words were in the old language, but it was a sad song, she could tell. As the fire died, the song echoed its dying. All the motherwitches were turned toward the singer, their faces lit by the flickering flames.

Very quietly, Anna drew close to the circle and sat down cross-legged behind her mother. As soon as the song was ended, she would whisper in her mother's ear, and then Ada Witch would make her visible again.

Suddenly the singing stopped. The singer looked up from the harp she held in her lap. "There is a hidden one among us," said the Old One. The motherwitches looked this way and that, but they could not see Anna Witch.

"Come here, little one," said the Old One, reaching out her bony hand. Slowly Anna

"The first round was disappearing," Anna went on. "I did that. But when it was my turn to make myself visible again, I couldn't. I tried, but I couldn't."

"So," said the Old One, and her voice was stern, "you have failed us twice. First, you played at magic, forgetting that the old wisdom is not to be played with. Then you failed us again, more seriously, with your lack of knowledge. Have you not been instructed?"

Anna stood silently, not knowing how to answer.

The Old One turned to Ada Witch. "The little one seems to have no answer. Perhaps the bats have stolen her tongue."

"My daughter is still very young," said Ada Witch softly. "She has not yet caught the spark of magic."

"She seems strong and healthy for her age," said the Old One. "I recall her birth. Is she not attentive to her lessons?"

"She tries to learn," said Ada Witch. "She practices her magic every day."

"Perhaps she does not understand how important it is that the old wisdom not be lost," said the Old One. "Each of us is a link in the chain of wisdom and power. That chain makes us all one, and a loss to one is a loss to all."

"I know that," said Ada Witch.

"You must make your daughter understand it, then," said the Old One. She turned to Anna Witch. "You must promise me that you will not let the chain be broken."

"I am sure Anna understands," said Ada Witch. "I shall take her home now and put her to bed. Come, Anna, help me gather up our things."

"Let the little one speak for herself," said the Old One, turning to Anna again. "Let me hear her promise."

"I promise," said Anna Witch, looking down at the ground.

"Very well, then," said the Old One. "You may go."

# CHAPTER 6

The next morning, after breakfast, Ada Witch got out the big book of magic earlier than usual. She had a very serious look on her face as she laid the book on the table.

"Anna," she said, "I am not going to scold you about last night, but I was very much embarrassed."

Anna Witch hung her head and said nothing.

"I don't understand it," Ada Witch went on. "A daughter of mine who cannot do magic. I know you could do it if you would only try."

"I do try," said Anna Witch. "It's too hard."

"Well," said Ada Witch, "perhaps it's my fault. Perhaps I haven't explained it well enough. Or perhaps I've tried to go too fast. So we're going to make a fresh start."

Ada Witch opened the big black book to the very first page. She had decided to teach Anna the easiest magic trick there is: how to create a spider from a pinch of salt. First she read the spell out loud.

"Salt wanders, spider ponders.
Spider creeps, salt sleeps.
Salt falls, spider crawls.
Spider knows, salt goes."

Then Ada Witch read all the directions to Anna and explained them step by step. Then they read the spell out loud together.

"Now watch exactly what I do," said Ada Witch, taking a pinch of salt and transforming it into a spider. "You see how simple it is, Anna?" she said. "Now watch me do it again." Ada Witch transformed the spider back into a pinch of salt, then into a spider again, then back to a pinch of salt. It did look very easy.

"Now you try it," she said. She put the pinch of salt into the palm of Anna's hand.

"I can't," said Anna.

"Just *try,* dear," her mother said.

"I can't," Anna repeated.

Otto was dozing on the mantelpiece, but even though his eyes were closed he knew what

was going on. "Can't or won't, Anna?" he said. "How do you know you can't until you try?"

"Anna is going to try," Ada Witch assured Otto. "She promised last night that she will try." Then she turned to her daughter. "I have lots of brewing to do today," she explained, "so I'm not going to watch you. You just sit here and practice the spell."

"How long do I have to practice?" Anna Witch grumbled.

"Until you get it right," her mother said, and went to stir up the fire under her big black pot.

"When can I go out?" asked Anna.

"When you get it right," said Otto, with his eyes closed.

So Anna Witch spent the morning sitting at the table practicing her magic. First she would whisper the spell over the pinch of salt, and then she would count silently to forty-nine, shutting her eyes each time she passed a seven. The next step is to blow on the pinch of salt, and it will change into a spider. It will, that is, if everything has been done correctly. But it was beginning to seem that Anna was not going to be very good at even this simple magic.

She kept looking out the window. It was a lovely day, and it was passing. She wanted to be out in the forest. But she had to keep practicing this stupid spell. After each failure, she looked out of the corner of her eye at Ada Witch, who seemed to be very busy at her caldron. Otto was fast asleep on the mantel. Then Anna would try the spell again. The whole morning had passed this way, and she still hadn't managed to change even one pinch of salt into a spider. She was just about ready to cry.

This time when she blew on the pinch of salt

it turned into a marshmallow. Anna burst into tears.

"Witches don't cry, Anna," said her mother, looking up from the purple potion she was stirring in her pot.

Otto flapped off the mantelpiece and plopped down on the table next to Anna. "I'll take that marshmallow," he said. "It looks very tasty."

"But I didn't want to create a marshmallow," cried Anna Witch. "I was trying to create a spider. Why is it that nothing I do ever turns out right?"

"If at first you don't succeed, try, try again," said Otto, swallowing the marshmallow.

"Do try it again, dear," said Ada Witch. "And this time *think* before you blow."

Anna took another pinch of salt and started over again from the beginning. When she had counted to forty-nine she tried to think. Had she done every step right? Would the pinch of salt turn into a spider this time? Or would it just blow away? She opened her eyes.

"Oh, I give up," she said in a loud, angry voice. "I don't want to create a spider anyhow."

"But don't you see, dear," her mother said patiently, "you have to learn this first. Then, when you've learned to create the spider, you can go on and create all kinds of other things. Marvelous things."

"I don't want to create anything," said Anna, stamping her little chicken foot.

"All witches must learn how to do magic," Ada Witch said firmly. "Who ever heard of a witch who couldn't cast a spell?"

"Then I don't want to be a witch," said Anna. She was getting quite green in the face with anger. "I hate doing spells."

"Remember what the Old One said, Anna. Each of us is a link in the chain."

"I don't care what the Old One says," Anna

answered. "I hate doing magic, and I'm not going to do it anymore. I'm never going to do even one more spell, so there!" And with that she picked up the big magic book and threw it across the room.

Ada Witch never lost her temper, but Anna could see that she was very angry. "Pick up that book, Anna," she said. "That book was handed down to us by your great-great-great-great-grandmother."

"I don't care," said Anna. "I won't pick it up. I won't do anything you say."

"All witches obey their mothers," said Ada Witch quietly.

"I wish I didn't have any mother," Anna shouted.

"Be careful what you wish, Anna," said Otto, who was still perched on the table. "Remember, a witch's wish is likely to come true."

"Anna," said Ada Witch, and her voice was so soft now that Anna began to be afraid of what might happen next, "pick up that book. I am warning you for the last time."

"I won't," said Anna. The more frightened she was by what she was doing, the more loudly she talked. And the longer she listened to her own angry voice, the angrier she felt. "I won't! And if you don't leave me alone, I'll put a spell on you. I'll turn you into a frog, that's what I'll do!"

Otto laughed. Anna turned on him. "What are you laughing at, you old bundle of feathers?"

"Do you really think you know how to turn someone into a frog, Anna?" Otto asked.

"Of course I do," she snapped. She was so angry that suddenly she did know. It came back to her in a flash exactly how Ada Witch had taught her to draw the special pattern through the air, and she remembered every word of the spell.

Shutting her eyes and carefully waving her clenched fists above her head in the correct manner, she recited:

"Turn to right, turn to left,
Turn together newt and eft.
Slimy marsh and muddy bog,
Turn from person into frog."

When she opened her eyes, a little green frog was sitting in the middle of the floor. And her mother was gone.

Anna didn't say anything. The little green frog didn't say anything either. And then the

frog turned away and slowly hopped through the house and out of the door.

"Now see what you've done," said Otto, shaking his head. "Remember what I said about a witch's wish."

# CHAPTER 7

Anna Witch felt very strange indeed. All of a sudden, everything had changed, and yet nothing was happening to her. She had done the worst thing she could think of, but she wasn't being punished. Even Otto didn't seem to be very angry. He wasn't really scolding her.

Perhaps, she thought, none of it had really happened. Perhaps she hadn't really transformed her mother into a little green frog. Perhaps in a minute the door would open and Ada Witch would come walking in. Otto interrupted her thoughts.

"If you'll excuse me, Anna, I think I'll get back to sleep," he said. "Early to bed and late to rise makes an owl healthy, wealthy, and wise, you know." With that he flew up into the rafters of the gingerbread house, fluffed up his brown feathers, and promptly fell asleep.

Anna Witch went out and sat on the doorstep with her chin in her hands, trying to decide what to do next. She was hungry, but she couldn't have lunch because she didn't know how to call the little magic table. There was nobody to tell her what to do. There was nobody to take care of her. Anna Witch was alone.

But no, she would not be frightened, and she would not cry. Anna Witch reminded herself that she was a brave, strong witchdaughter. She didn't need anyone to take care of her; she could take care of herself. She didn't need the little magic table; there were plenty of candy decorations on the gingerbread house for her to eat. And she most certainly did not need anyone to tell her what to do. From now on, she would do whatever she pleased.

In fact, she would start right now. Instead of sitting on the doorstep feeling lonely, she would have a nice lunch. After that, she would go out into the forest and invite some of the animals she liked best to a party. They would all celebrate the first day of Anna Witch's freedom.

This idea cheered Anna up right away. And getting ready for the party gave her a lot to do. First she brought out the best lace tablecloth

wished they had time, but they needed all day to catch enough worms and bugs for their babies. The moles were terribly sorry, but they had to put their children to bed.

Just as Anna Witch was deciding to give up and go home, a small brown rabbit came popping out from behind a bush. "I heard you're having a party at the gingerbread house," the rabbit said.

"That's true," admitted Anna Witch.

"Can I come to your party?" whined the little rabbit. "I've never been to a party."

Anna looked at the rabbit doubtfully. She had never seen this particular rabbit before, but it seemed very much like all the others she knew. Anna Witch had never met a rabbit yet who had anything interesting to say, and they always hopped about so fast and wiggled their noses so much that being with them made her feel rather nervous.

On the other hand, any guest at all was surely better than none. "All right," she said. "Come along."

"I have lots of brothers and sisters at home," said the little rabbit, its whiskers twitching eagerly. "They'd like to come, too."

Anna considered the idea. After all, she had

set six places. "I could take four of them," she offered. "Where are they?"

"Wait right here," said the young rabbit, and popped down a nearby hole Anna had not noticed before.

Anna Witch sat down to wait. She waited and waited. What was taking so long? She was afraid her flower chains were wilting.

Then from the hole poured the rabbit family. There seemed to be a great many of them. The mother rabbit came hopping over to Anna. "I'm sorry it's taken so long to get them all cleaned up," she said, extending a paw. "It's so very kind of you to invite them to your party. It will give me a chance to get a bit of rest. You have no idea what it's like to have so many children. Never a moment's peace. I sleep with one eye open."

"I'm afraid there's been a mistake," said Anna Witch timidly. "I'm only inviting five."

"Only five?" said the mother rabbit indignantly. "That would hardly be fair. How do you think all the others would feel, being left out? No, no, either they all go or none of them do." She glared at Anna.

All the young rabbits began to squeal. Anna had to shout to make herself heard over their cries. "All right, all right," she said. "I'll take them all. Just make them be quiet."

The little rabbits quieted down instantly. "That's better," said the mother rabbit. "Now let me introduce you."

One by one, the little rabbits came forward to shake Anna Witch's hand. Their names turned out to be Caroline, Carl, Cobina, Clarissa, Conrad, Constanzia, Charles, Cora, and Cary. "You'll notice that their names all begin with C," said the mother rabbit proudly. "That's because we belong to the oldest, most aristocratic branch of the cony family. See how long their ears are, how fluffy their tails. They are all very distinguished looking, aren't they?"

"And what's the smallest one's name?" asked Anna politely, pointing to the little rabbit she had met first.

"Oh, he doesn't have a name," his mother answered. "I couldn't think of another nice name beginning with C."

Anna did not know what to say to this. She had never known anyone who did not have a name. "You must call him *something,*" she objected.

"If you're really having a party, you should get started," suggested the mother rabbit, mov-

ing toward the rabbit hole. "It's terribly late in the day for growing children to have their lunch."

The young rabbits began to squeal again. Jumping up and down, they cried "Let's go!" and "We want our lunch!"

"You see?" said their mother, looking reproachfully back at Anna. "The poor little things are hungry."

Anna wondered if she had enough to feed all these hungry rabbits. What if there weren't enough candy decorations to keep them satisfied? What would they do? And then she thought of Ada Witch's herb garden. She remembered that her mother had always told her how much rabbits love gardens. And she remembered how many times her mother had warned her to latch the gate carefully to be sure no rabbits would ever come near the tender green herbs.

Anna Witch did not want to hurt the mother rabbit's feelings, but she had to bring the subject up. "There's just one thing before we go," she began. "There's something at our house that your children must stay away from. They must promise to leave it alone or they can't come."

The mother rabbit seemed quite offended. "I don't know what you have at your house, since I've never been there," she said stiffly, "but I'm sure my children know the right way to behave anywhere."

"I'm glad to hear that," said Anna, "because my mother would be very upset if they got into her garden."

"Garden?" said the mother rabbit excitedly. "Do you mean to tell me that you have a garden? Imagine that! My mother told me that an old aunt of hers lived near the village, and she saw a garden. I've been hearing about that garden all my life, and I've told the children, too, but I never thought I'd live to see one! If you have a garden, I'll change my mind and come to your party myself!"

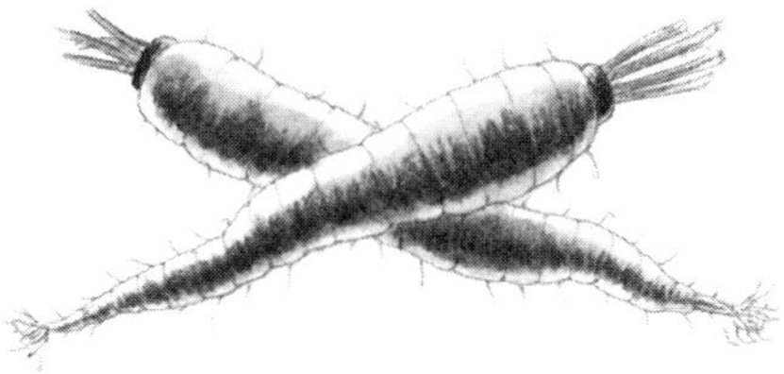

# CHAPTER 8

The rabbits hopped so fast that Anna had to hurry to keep up, and some of them reached the gate in the picket fence before Anna got there. But, of course, they had to wait for Anna Witch to open the little magic gate by whispering to it.

Before she opened the gate, Anna looked at her guests. She thought it was wise to ask for one last promise.

"They won't get into the garden, will they?" Anna Witch asked the mother rabbit.

"Of course they won't," she answered. "I've brought them up to have perfect manners."

The first thing the rabbits saw as they rushed through the gate was the lace tablecloth spread on the grass. All the party things were ar-

ranged neatly on it, just as Anna Witch had left them. Even the flower chains were hardly wilted at all. Everything looked very inviting.

"Food," squealed all the young rabbits, racing toward it.

"Wait," said Anna. "I'll have to rearrange things a little. I only set six places."

"Never mind about that," said the mother rabbit. "We don't care." And with that, she jumped into the middle of the tablecloth, among the dishes and flower chains. All the little rabbits followed her example.

When Anna Witch had planned her party, she had imagined her guests sitting sedately around the edges of the cloth, eating politely with knife and fork. First they would all admire the pretty cloth and the flower decorations. Then they would have pleasant conversation as they ate. And afterward they would play games. But things were not going as she had planned.

The whole tablecloth was swarming with rabbits. There were rabbits snatching and grabbing, rabbits chewing and swallowing, rabbits guzzling and chomping. All Anna could hear was the sound of crunching and munching.

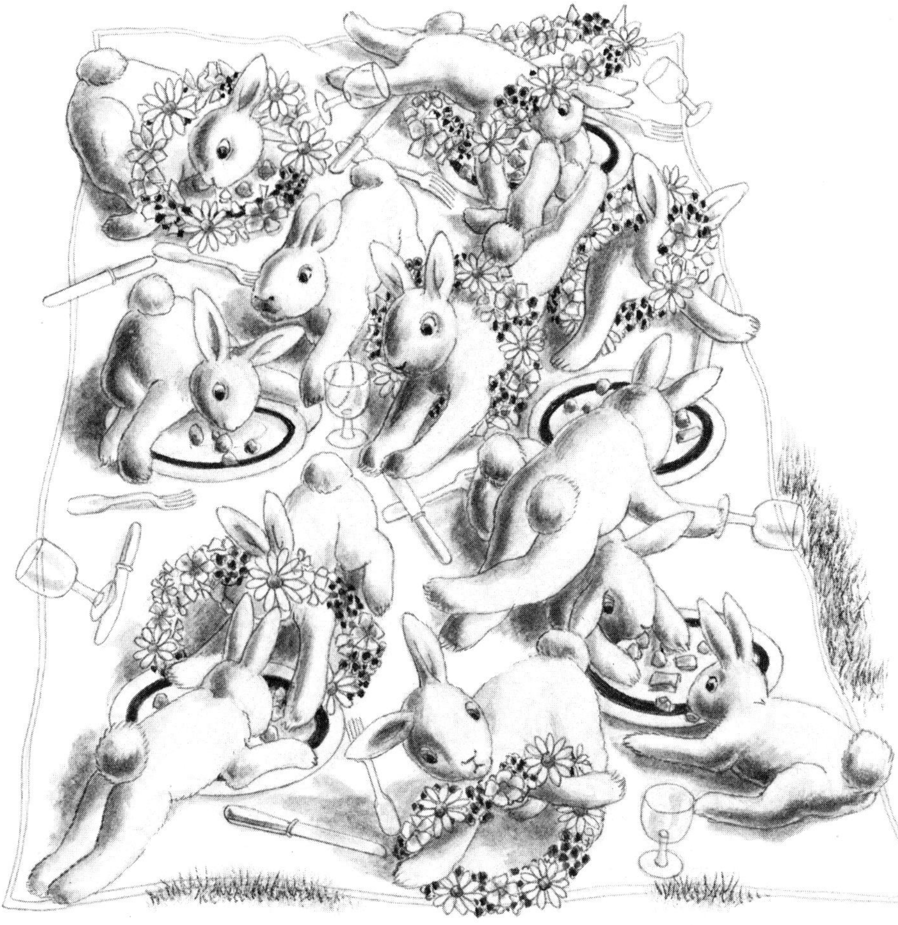

In a few minutes every scrap had been eaten, even the flower chains. "What else have you got to eat?" cried the young rabbits. "We're hungry!"

"Nothing at all," said Anna Witch firmly. "You've had enough. It's time to play games now."

"They don't want to play games," the mother rabbit said. "They want to see the garden now."

"Remember, you promised," said Anna. "You promised they wouldn't touch it."

"They're not going to hurt it," the mother rabbit assured Anna. "They only want to see it."

All the rabbits followed Anna around to the back of the house where Ada Witch's herb garden was. For the first time, they stopped jumping around nervously and really paid attention. They stood at the edge of the garden and closed their eyes. They all took deep breaths.

"It's just as I always imagined it would be," exclaimed the mother rabbit. "Just as my mother described it. She told me her aunt had a carrot once. Do you have carrots in this garden?"

"I don't think so," said Anna. "I don't think I've ever seen one. What do they look like?"

"A carrot," explained the mother rabbit dreamily, "is one of the most beautiful things in the world. It's of a lovely orange color, and its leaves are like green feathers. And the taste is simply indescribable. My mother's aunt always told her she would never forget it, not if she lived to be twenty years old."

"We don't have anything like that," said Anna. "This garden has nothing but the herbs my mother uses to make her magic potions."

"But the beautiful orange part is underground," argued the mother rabbit. "The only part you see aboveground is the green leaves. And I think I see one growing right there. Yes, I'm quite sure all those plants are carrots."

"I'm sure they're not," said Anna.

One of the little rabbits was whispering something into his mother's long ear.

"Well, of course," said the mother rabbit. "Of course, he wants you to pull one up so they can see what a carrot looks like."

"You promised they'd leave the garden alone," protested Anna.

"I cannot believe the selfishness of it," sighed

the mother rabbit. "You have so many, surely you could spare *one*. All their lives they've heard about carrots, and now to be so close and not even see one. Look at those sad little faces. It's enough to melt a heart of stone."

Anna did not feel her heart melting as she looked at the faces of the young rabbits. They did not look at all sad. They looked greedy. Their noses were wiggling, their whiskers were twitching.

"Just one," they all squealed. "Just one!"

Reluctantly, Anna reached down and pulled up one of the plants. It didn't look at all like the mother rabbit's description of what a carrot should be. Its root wasn't even orange. It was white and covered with dirt. But all the rabbits gathered around eagerly. Suddenly the smallest one, the one with no name, snatched the plant from Anna's hand. In a trice he had crunched it down, dirt and all.

All the other little rabbits began to squeal. "Now you must let the others have one, too," said the mother rabbit, turning to Anna Witch. "It's not fair to let one of them have a carrot and not the others."

"I didn't give it to him, and it wasn't a carrot," said Anna. "I think it was comfrey."

"Well, whatever it was," said the mother rabbit, "it's only fair to let them all have one."

The little rabbits were squeaking and squealing more loudly than ever. Anna Witch put her hands over her ears. "All right," she shouted, trying to make herself heard. "They can each have one when they leave." Suddenly there was silence among the rabbits.

The mother rabbit looked at the sky. "It's

their clothes were much too big. Their hats slid down to the rabbits' noses.

"I'll be the mother," announced one of the rabbits.

"No, I'm the mother," protested the other. "I'm bigger. You can be Anna Witch."

"I don't want to. Who wants to be Anna Witch?" the smaller one said, reaching out to pull her sister's whiskers. Her sister knocked off the hat she was wearing. They both began to squeak with fury.

Anna was afraid the noisy rabbits would wake up Otto. Was he still asleep? Could he sleep in all this racket? He wasn't used to that during the day.

And what would he say if he woke up? Rabbits inside the fence, rabbit footprints on the lace tablecloth and all around the garden. And now, rabbits even in the house. Rabbits all dressed up like witches, quarreling with each other. Oh, if Ada Witch could see this, how very angry she would be.

Anna picked up the two rabbits by the ears and knocked their heads together. The petticoats they were wearing slipped off. Then she carried them out of the house and put them

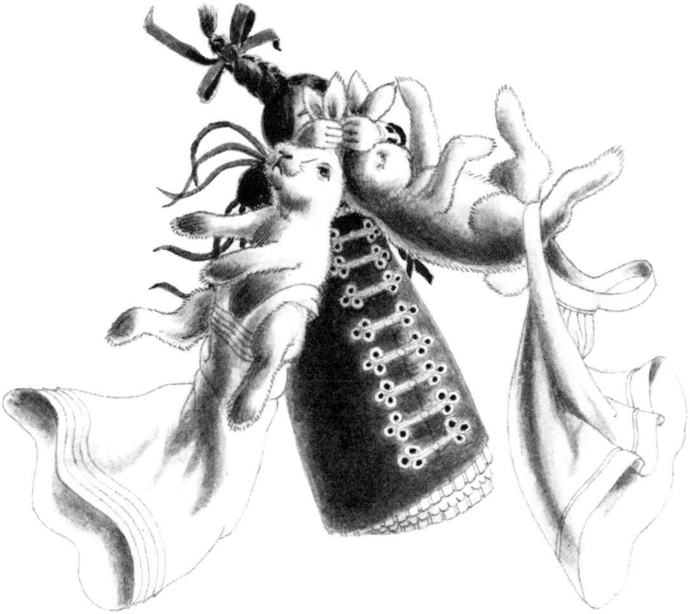

down hard outside the gate. They were too frightened even to squeal.

"Go home now," said Anna Witch sternly, as she latched the gate again. "And don't come back until you learn some manners."

Then she went back to the house. First she washed the dishes. Then she put everything away neatly. She even picked up the big magic book from where it lay on the floor, and returned it to its own special shelf.

The sun was setting by this time, and when it began to grow dark Otto woke up from his day-long sleep. He sat and watched as Anna Witch lit the candles.

"I see you've had a bad day," he said at last. "You look very disappointed."

Anna Witch did not want to admit that he was right. "I didn't have a bad day at all," she said. "I've just given a very successful garden party."

"But you didn't enjoy it," Otto said. "You missed your mother. Remember, I warned you to be careful what you wished."

"You're quite wrong," said Anna Witch crossly. She did not like having Otto guess what she was thinking. "I had a wonderful day. I may give another party tomorrow."

"All right," said the owl. "You know best how you feel. If you tell me you're happy, I must take your word. And now good night, Anna. I'm on my way down to the frog pond to pay a little call on your mother. Is there anything you'd like me to tell her?"

"No," said Anna Witch, turning her back on him. "Just go."

# CHAPTER 9

Anna Witch went to the window and watched Otto flapping away through the trees. She felt very sorry for herself, all alone in the house with not even an owl to talk to.

As she sat by the window, the sun sank lower and lower until it completely disappeared, and the sky grew dark. The stars came out. It was night now, and as she watched she began to see witches flying, first one by one and two by two, over the treetops. Soon all the witches for miles around were on their way to the mountaintop. Big and little, through the stars they flew, swooping, gliding, and circling on their swift brooms.

Anna Witch looked out the window until the moon came up and from the distant mountaintop she could see the witches' bonfire begin to glow. Now she knew they were dancing and singing, and all the witchdaughters were in the pine grove, laughing and jumping their snakes, and twirling with joy. Only Anna was all alone.

Could she ever go to the mountaintop again? They would ask her where her mother was, and how could she answer that? She could never lie to them. If she tried that, she knew the Old One would grasp her by the arm with her cold, bony hand, and look deep into her eyes. She would have to tell the whole story then. And how could she tell the Old One that her mother was now just a little green frog down in the pond?

And when the witches knew the truth, not one of them—not a motherwitch, not a witchdaughter—would ever speak to her again. She was an outcast. She would never again go to the midnight picnic, never again dance as a true daughter of the Great First Mother around the sacred fire. She would have to live alone for the rest of her life, alone in the little house deep in the forest. No one would ever come to see her. No one would even know she lived there. Even Otto would fly away from her.

Anna climbed up the ladder into her little bed and pulled the quilt up over her head. But she could not sleep. She tossed and turned. She tried counting imaginary animals to put herself to sleep. First she tried counting squirrels running, one after another, into a hollow tree. But as she tried to picture them in her mind, their ears grew longer and their tails shorter, and she didn't want to think about rabbits.

It would be better not to count furry animals of any kind. She started to count imaginary turtles jumping, one by one, off a fallen log into the water. But the water reminded her of the frog pond, and she didn't want to think about that either.

She decided to think about nothing at all. She lay very still and thought hard about nothing at all for what seemed a very long time. And still she could not sleep. She began to wonder if she would ever be able to sleep again. At last she heard the swish of feathers at the window and the sound of an owl thumping down on a shelf. Otto had come back.

Anna sat up in bed and opened the curtains.

There was Otto, reaching into the jar where Ada Witch kept his favorite seedcakes.

"Anna," Otto said in his gruff voice, "you should be asleep."

"I couldn't sleep," said Anna. "Why are you so late for supper?"

"I was having such an interesting discussion with your mother in the frog pond," Otto explained. "A sparkling conversationalist, your mother."

"What is she doing down there in the frog pond, Otto?" Anna dared to ask. "Isn't it muddy and cold down there?"

"Not to a frog, Anna," said the owl. "And now that she is a frog, she's very popular down at the pond, very much in demand. The frogs like to sing in the evenings, you know, and your mother has always been noted for her lovely voice."

"But . . . but doesn't she want to come home, Otto?" Anna said in her smallest voice. "I mean, doesn't she miss me? Didn't she even ask you how I was?"

"Of course she did. A mother is always a mother, even if she is a frog. But I told her you were very happy without her."

"But that's not true, Otto!" Anna protested.

"Isn't that what you told me?"

"Yes," cried Anna, "but you knew perfectly well it wasn't true! You knew I couldn't go to bed without my own mother to tuck me in and give me a kiss and sing me a little witchaby before I go to sleep!"

Suddenly, with a hop and a skip up the ladder, a little green frog jumped onto Anna's pillow. Anna Witch wanted to throw her arms around her mother's neck and tell her how glad

she was to see her again, but it is hard to throw your arms around a frog's neck.

"Oh, please turn back into my mother again," she begged.

"Perhaps she prefers to be a frog," said Otto. "But she is still your mother, no matter what her shape is."

"A frog mother is better than no mother at all," said Anna, "but I like her real shape best."

"If she wanted to change, she would," said Otto. "Don't you think a powerful witch like your mother can take any shape she wants?"

"A witchchild needs a witchmother," said Anna Witch firmly. "Not a frog." Suddenly her eye fell on the big magic book. It was lying on its special shelf where she had put it that very afternoon, as thick and black and heavy as ever. The gold letters on its cover shone softly in the candlelight.

Down the ladder climbed Anna, quick as a dragonfly, and ran to the bookshelf, the little green frog hopping along behind her. Rapidly turning the pages, Anna Witch found the spell she was looking for.

Very slowly, holding her breath all the while, Anna Witch walked in a triangle around the little green frog. Pointing both her thumbs at the frog and looking straight into its eyes, she recited the spell:

"Turn to left, turn to right,
Fading day must turn to night.
Caldron bubble and fire burn,
To your natural shape return!"

Then, not letting her glance waver for a moment, she began to say the alphabet backward, starting from Z. "Z," said Anna softly, unblinking. "Y, X, W."

And as she spoke, a haze began to gather in